NOTE: The small pictures that are printed to the upper right of some signs are suffixes. These include plurals, -ing and the possessive. Sign the suffix immediately after the root-word sign, as shown.

Use lots of facial expression, and always speak when signing.

The alphabet on the inside back cover will make many signs clearer. Hand-positions often represent the first letter of the word signed (e.g. "dad" — "D" and "big" — "B") For additional clarification, a glossary is printed at the back of the book which gives the description of how each sign is produced.

Modern Signs Press, Inc., solicits your comments and suggestions.

I WAS SO MAD!!

WRITTEN AND ILLUSTRATED
BY JONI HERIGSTAD

| Shelly | and | I | had |

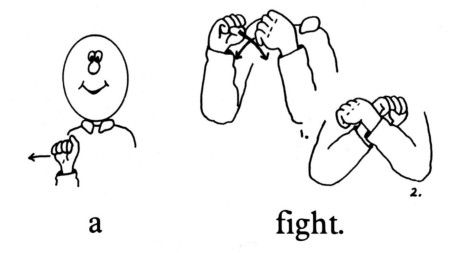

| a | fight. |

I   was   so   mad!!

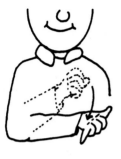

Shelly

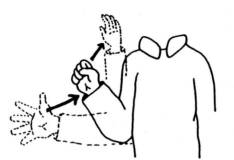

took

my

new

doll.

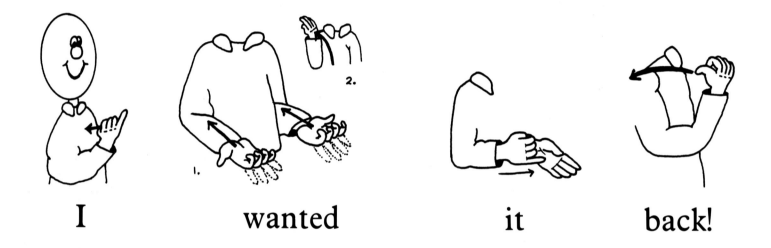

I   wanted   it   back!

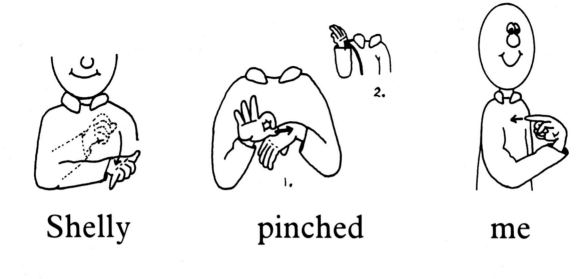

Shelly   pinched   me

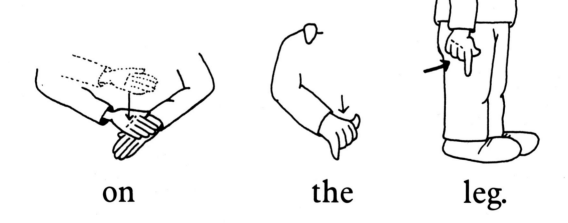

on   the   leg.

So   I   pinched

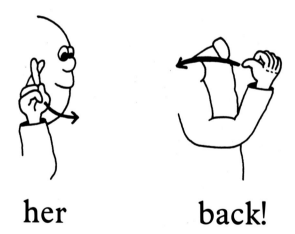

her   back!

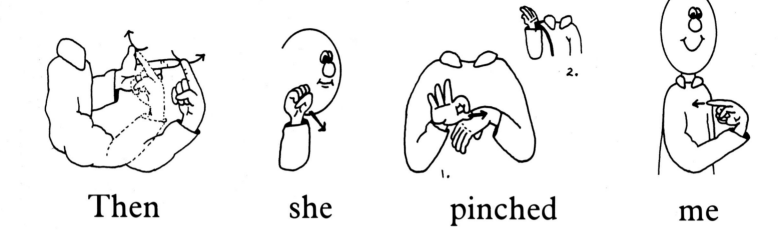

Then   she   pinched   me

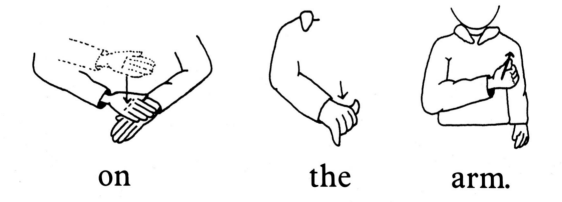

on   the   arm.

So   I   pinched

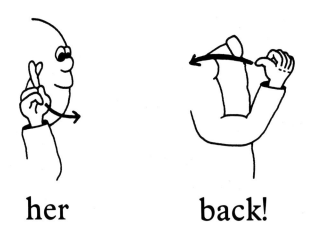

her   back!

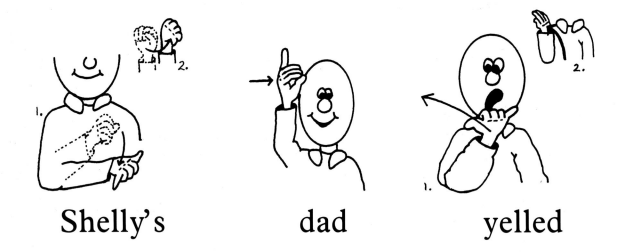

Shelly's   dad   yelled

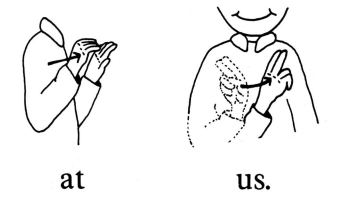

at   us.

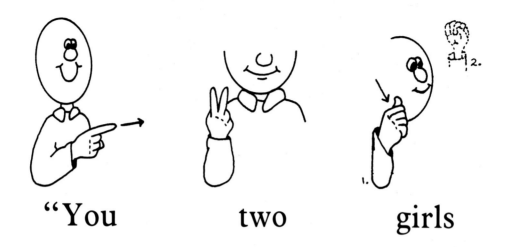

"You   two   girls

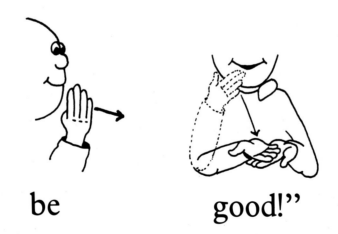

be   good!"

I   was   so   mad!!

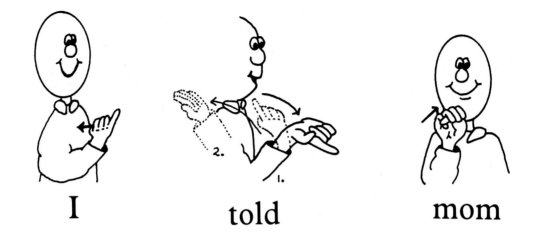

I   told   mom

  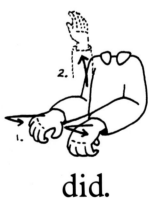

what   Shelly   did.

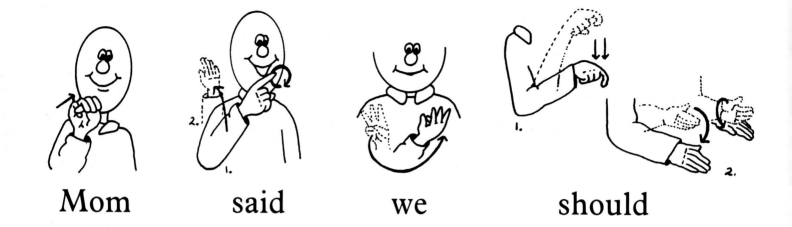

Mom   said   we   should

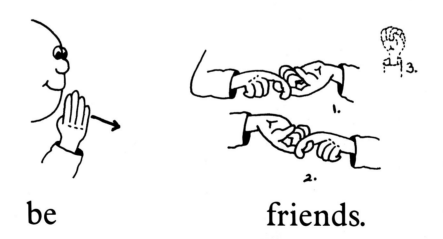

be   friends.

The   next   day

I   saw   Shelly.

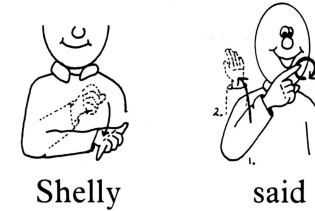

Shelly

said

she

was

sorry.

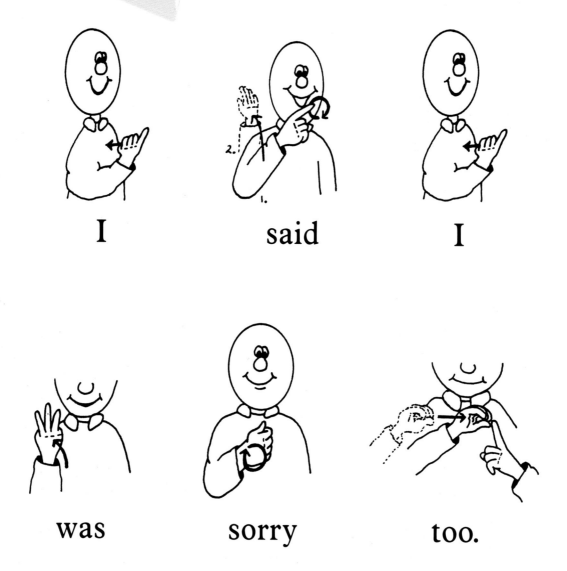

I said I

was sorry too.

So   now   we're

friends   again!

GLOSSARY

A - Palm-out A moves slightly right

AGAIN - Strike heel of left hand with bent right fingertips

AND - Palm-in, 5-hand, pulls to right, closing to a flat-O

ARM - Pat arm with A

AT - Right fingertips approach and touch back of left fingers

BACK - Extended-A thumb jerks back over shoulder

BE - B below lips; move forward

DAD - D touches temple

DAY - Right 1-hand drops down on left arm

DID=(DO+Past-Tense) - Palm-down C-hands move side-to-side; palm of right hand flips back toward shoulder

DOLL - Right X-finger brushes off tip of nose

FIGHT - S-hands face each other, jerk to cross at wrists; repeat

FRIEND(S) - Index fingers hook, first right over left, then left over right, add palm-out S hand

GIRL(S) - Thumb of extended-A hand moves down jawline, add palm-out S-hand

GOOD - Palm-in fingers on chin, drop to palm of left hand

HAD=(HAVE+Past-Tense) - Fingertips of slightly bent hands approach and touch chest, palm of right hand flips back toward shoulder

HER - Palm-out R slides down jawline forward

I - Palm-left I-hand touches chest

IT - Tip of I touches palm of left hand

LEG - L-hand pats thigh

MAD - 5-hand in front of face contract to claw

ME - Index points to and touches chest

MOM - M taps near chin

MY - Flat hand palm on chest

NEW - Palm-up right hand arcs down, brushes across left palm, and arcs up slightly

NEXT - Flat hands, palms in; back hand jumps to front

NOW - Palm-up bent hands slightly drop

ON - Right palm touches back of left hand

PINCH(ED) - Thumb slips past tip of index while resting on back of left hand (takes a pinch), palm of right hand flips back toward shoulder

SAID=(SAY+Past-Tense) - Index circles up and outward near mouth, palm of right hand flips back toward shoulder

SAW=(SEE+Past-Tense) - Palm-in V from eye outward, palm of right hand flips back toward shoulder

SHE - Palm-out E slides along jawline and forward

SHELLY (Name Sign) - S-hand on chest, drops to a Y-hand

SHOULD - Palm-down X nods, then flat hands, palms facing, drop to palms-down

SO - Right S moves sharply down, striking side of left S in passing

SORRY - A circles on chest

THE - Palm-down Y drops slightly

THEN - Index moves from off left thumb to off tip of left index

TOLD=(TELL+Past Tense) - Palm-down index under chin flips out to palm-up

TOO - O approaches and touches left index

TOOK=(TAKE+Past-Tense) - 5-hand draws back toward body, closing to S, palm of right hand flips back toward shoulder

TWO - First two fingers, V shape, palm-in

US - U at right side of chest circles to left side

WANT(ED) - Palms-up, 5's pull back to claws toward body, palm of right hand flips back toward shoulder

WAS - Palm-in W moves back toward right shoulder

WE - W on right side of chest circles to left side

WE('RE) - W on right side of chest circles to left side, palm-out R twists inward

WHAT - Index fingertip brushes down across left fingers

YELL(ED) - Palm-in Y moves up and out from chin, palm of right hand flips back toward shoulder

YOU - Index points at person addressed

DRAW AND COLOR A PICTURE OF JILL

DRAW AND COLOR A PICTURE OF SHELLY PLAYING